Change is scary. It's scary to start a new job. It's scary in the first few post-honeymoon days of a marriage. Hell, kindergarten is scary. Still, the most admired artists are the ones most willing to grow and surprise us. And yet, we sense that the artist in late career contains all of his/her younger selves.

I've been reading Larry Smith's work for over 20 years. That's long enough to make his work seem like it's always been there, and maybe that's because the people Larry writes about are ones I recognize: mill workers and farmers, waitresses and librarians. He writes about family and everyday concerns. Sometimes those are scrambled eggs. Sometimes they are snow birds. Sometimes love, sometimes death. He is a tactile and empathetic poet.

This new book shows someone who is not afraid to grow, even after many books. Along with his sparks of Zen, there's a joyful surrealism here. Even the most black and white, photographic poems don't take themselves too seriously and genuinely open us.

Smith's people spend a lot of time waiting. They wait for money, for night, or for the dark laughter of an epiphany to hit as a hard as "a busload of bibles." These poems exist right outside of town in a peddler's encampment where fairy tales and bad luck mingle with white bread and pennies. These are magical riddles made up of the real and the nearly so. Feast on them and dance.

~ Mike James, author of *Crows in the Jukebox*

Other Books by Larry Smith

Fiction:
The Free Farm: A Novel (Bottom Dog Press, 2011).
The Long River Home: A Novel (Bottom Dog Press, 2009).
Faces and Voices: Tales (Bird Dog Publishing, 2007).
Working It Out (Ridgeway Press, 1998).
Beyond Rust (Bottom Dog Press, 1995).

Memoirs:
The Thick of Thin: Memoirs of a Working-Class Writer (Bottom Dog Press   2015).
Milldust and Roses (Ridgeway Press, 2002).

Poetry:
Lake Winds: Poems (Bottom Dog Press, 2014).
each moment all: Poems (March Street Press, 2011).
Tu Fu Comes to America: A Story in Poems (March Street Press 2010, rev. 2018).
A River Remains (WordTech Editions, 2006).
Thoreau's Lost Journal (Westron Press 2002, rev. 2017).
Steel Valley: Postcards & Letters (Pig Iron Press, 1992).
Across These States (Bottom Dog Press, 1985).
Scissors, Paper, Rock (Cleveland State University Poetry Center, 1982).
Echo Without Sound: Poems by Larry Smith, Etchings by Stephen Smigocki (Northwood Press, 1981).
Growth: Poems (Northwood Press, (1975).

Biography & Nonfiction:
Images of America: Mingo Junction, co-edited with Guy Mason (Arcadia Publishing, 2011).
Lawrence Ferlinghetti: Poet-At-Large (Southern Illinois University Press, 1983).
Kenneth Patchen: Rebel Poet in America (A Consortium of Small Presses, 2000; rev. 2013).

Films (Written and co-produced with Tom Koba):
James Wright's Ohio (1988).
Kenneth Patchen: An Art of Engagement (1989).

THE PEARS
POEMS

LARRY SMITH

"When they ask for apples,
give them pears."
~Charles Simic

Harmony Poetry Series
Bottom Dog Press
Huron, OH

Credits
Cover art by Nitr from Shutterstock
Cover Layout and Design by Susanna Sharp-Schwacke

Acknowledgments

A special thanks to Mike James for his guidance on this collection
and to the members of the Firelands Writing Center for their sharing.
And to wife Ann for sharing them early and offering encouragement.
I am particularly endebted to the inspiring work of Charles Simic
and Kenenth Patchen in this volume.

Thanks to the following who published many of these poems in
2018-2019:
"A Work Story" in *Live Nude Poems*, July 2019.
"Lost and Found" in *The Rye Whiskey Review* December, 2018; "The
Passage," "The Roma—Gypsies," and "Detroit Conception," forth-
coming in 2019.
"Wages" and "No Walls" in *As It Ought To Be Magazine* 2019; "Forget
Math and Science,"forthcoming in 2019.
"Getting the Message" in *Unbroken*, April 2019.
"The Making" in *Bidwell Hollow*, 2019.

Contents

The Writing

Don't go running off to
pick out a cut tree
then bring it into the house
and load it with gaudy decorations.

Dig a small one from the earth at night
and drag it along the ground,
then pot and place it on the porch
leaves and bugs and all
where rain and snow can feed it.

Part One

anyone lived in a pretty how town
(with up so floating many bells down)
~ e. e. cummings

The Pears

"O taste and see."

the pears must be eaten
before the day is through
a skin of feet
pressed to the lips
broken and entered
by the tongue of light

sweet taste
a long thread of memory
wrapped round the fingers
of forgetting

apples into oranges
peaches into plums
the pears

The Making

A circle of poets sits round a fire,
a dozen at times, tonight maybe eight.
They sit on old logs or in the cool sand
with a halfmoon overhead.
Each is eager to break silence
with words spoken into the night.

One woman rocks a baby that's not there,
another holds a doll in her lap that is her.
Two men hold each other and rock back and forth.
An old man leans forward, his hand on his heart,
his eyes closed as he speaks into the silence.

The young girl has had her guitar removed
and sits outside the circle in curses.
A virgin poet begins to recite an old poem
and is stopped, "Not now," an elder says.
"This is the making, not the showing."
A woman in long gray hair touches his arm
and says for all, "It's the very best part."

Forgetting Math and Science

Birds live inside of birds
tucked away for spring release
their naked bodies embraced
in sleep's sweet curve.
Their wings are tongues licking
each other's face.
Don't try to count them all;
they're an infinite multiple of six.

To love a single bird
you must become one
inside and out, top to bottom.
Awaken wings and rise to fly
sing through beak and body
the song of I Am.

The Roma—Gypsies

Can that be—smoke shooting out
of that woman's breasts?
It pulls the eyes up to the sky
then back to the empty space
where a beautiful girl had been.
My skin burns, my legs shake.
A Ferris wheel rolls off the cliff
into Lake waters, where
heads and bottoms bob.

Who has driven these people here
from what distant lands?
Who will drive them away again?

A wild smoke of violins and wine
attaches to your lungs.
Bright shirts and flowered skirts
lie spread across the lawn,
while the wheel of fortune turns.
You swallow a breath.
You close your eyes to see.

Atlantic City Collage

The old hotel at the boardwalk edge
grays like the back of your hair.
Too many children have run through its doors
begging for bread and eggs.

Tall glasses of water rock on the shelf
as horses drop from wooden platforms
into blue buckets of water.
A Ferris wheel kisses the sky.

They say my grandfather slept on the sand,
too cheap to pay for hotel sheets.
At dusk they washed in the ocean.
At dawn they ate what they'd brought.

Grandmother would remember
and cry when she laughed.
A fan blowing her hair
into a mask.

Buster Keaton Arcade

You wake to a phone call at midnight,
a woman screaming at breaking glass,
and you just lie there till it quiets.

Your daughter takes off on her new bike
circling the neighborhood with wings
and doesn't come back.

Two days you wait for your muffler
to fall off in the road, outside the diner
where Fish—Ice—Worms are served.

The postman casts our mail
across the wet grass,
for my dog and I to eat.

When the limb falls
in the stormy night
it strikes a busload of bibles.

Bathing in It

Lying in the warm waters of my bathtub
I close my eyes and walk into the River Ganges.
Flowers and filth floating round me,
in bright daylight I bathe with them,
their brown faces reflecting off my white.

The men smiling half naked, the women
wrapping bright cloth at their waist and thighs,
all pouring the dark waters on self and others.
One holds a child to the sky and all
lift prayer hands and voices.

On these same banks upriver are those
gathering around a burning body
offering prayers and loving presence.
I bow to my sisters and brothers.

Counting my breaths now back from twenty,
I lie in the gentleness of these waters
and sense the silence in their cries
of loss and loving. Oh, sweet life.
Oh, forgiveness.

Blind Perch Café

The old woman sitting near the window turns to me,
her face an ancient wallpaper, her eyes clouded marbles.
Is she dead? I think aloud and smell the waste of dogs.
The waitress refuses to appear, and so I sit
thinking of how I got here. Seems only yesterday
I delivered bibles to the penitentiary on the hill.
The prisoners would set up a murmur of approval
though I never saw their faces, just their hands.
A stone's throw from this café is the ditch
where the woman's body was found.

When the waitress appears at my side,
I order a pilsner and perch sandwich.
The waitress bends to spit in my face saying,
"Don't you know the name of this place!
We're here to preserve not to extinct."
Blind Perch…it all makes sense. *Blind perch*,
a creature handicapped yet honored here.
When I look at the waitress again
it is the dead woman's face.

Detroit Conception

They are writing a song, the four of them,
seated around an old church piano.
Outside the wind is pushing snow
along the dark city streets.
A pack of feral dogs look in the windows
thinking only of meat.

Mike at the piano runs through the chords.
A bottle is passed round.
For a moment only the wind, then suddenly
Janet rises, spreads her dark arms, and
words like notes bubble out as though
blown by a kid at a street fair.
The others watch her bare arms and hands
beckon them, then howl like the wolves outside
in a chorus of sweet longing. They will do this again
and again till they get it right,
then name it "Detroit Night."

Books: A Love Poem

You stand short and tall, Books,
or you lie, a picnic of words, spread
across a blanket old yet new.
In silence your call to life
opens the heart's eyes, the body's ears
before bulldozers of money and matter
would swallow all.

Books, you are a glass-bottom boat
reflecting the changing sky.

A song awaiting a singer,
you open to all voices and call:
Come devour me—but slowly
as thoughts flower in a field,
as sun daily glides into moon.

Sometimes I fold you, close eyes,
and press my hands to your face.

Part Two

We can walk into our separate sleep
on floors of music where the milkwhite cloak
of childhood lies
~ Kenneth Patchen

Getting the Message

I find Chinese writing on the bathroom mirror, a large scroll of a dozen characters. I don't write or read Chinese, and no one has been here in days. So much of life a mystery, and we the Emperor without clothes.

I take the mirror's photo and text it to Mei, my Chinese friend who now lives in Taiwan. It may be days before I hear back, and so I continue my routine of wasting, washing, shaving, brushing, as though the key to this secret will surely be delivered soon, like a package from the UPS.

Opening a book, watching a film, listening to a story—such hope and trust, so often betrayed.

Only once did my grandfather sit me down to tell his life story. Just a boy of eight sitting with him on their front porch swing, I listened unable to take it all in or to remember. We never spoke of it again. Years later, Mother told me he had been diagnosed with cancer and was to die soon. His secret remains a dream away.

Birds cry outside the window. I wipe the mirror with a wet cloth.

Christmas in Cleveland

We sleep standing up, my wife and I, in the cold hospital room of someone we don't really know.

Someone, a nurse probably, says it is God and leaves the room.
We bow our heads, leaning over Him to watch a glow brighten then dim, then brighten and dim again.

Outside the window, sirens sing on the streets as snow covers the night.
I go to look and see dogs gathered in the parking lot below without barking, just dogs looking up this way as if to ask why He is causing the snow.

I shrug my shoulders and wave them off, but they won't go.

I look over at my wife for answers, but she is already standing at the head of the bed, bending close to listen as deep groans rise.

Nothing, and then, the glow brightens greatly as she turns to me and says, "He says He's made mistakes. He asks us for forgiveness."

We both fall to our knees as though a new birth has come to the world.

The dogs begin to howl.

Eating Out

Somewhere someone is turning eggs in a pan.
I am seated with strangers who speak only German.
The noise is so loud, I just nod my head.
The waitress pours coffee or oil into my cup.
I smile and nod, while under the table
a line of black ants crosses the floor.
I have been here before, and now I'm back again.

The waitress has forgotten our silverware, and so
we eat in silence with our hands.
When I look up, my dead father
is sitting across the table. He leans back,
wipes his face and calls for the check.
Outside the building his train is waiting,
pulsing in the night, but we can't leave.
Our waitress has gone home
to be with her kids.

Facing It

A man parks his car on the county road.
He gets out and walks to the railroad tracks
where he lays across the rails and waits—
Who knows how long?

The engineer brakes, then closes his eyes.

I come upon the scene just minutes later.
Three panting diesels begin to stall.
Two emergency vehicles blare past me,
too late as well. Death is spread everywhere
and nowhere—Where to begin?

I read the story that night—not much.
He was 72, no family,
lived at the veterans' home.
Only the engineer speaks.
 "I saw him there. Couldn't stop.
We're a train—Good God,
we can't just make it stop."

And now I, at 75, can't stop either
wondering his last thoughts—
A mute blankness? Or perhaps,
like poet Miklos Radnoti—
shot then thrown in a mass grave—
Acceptance? "Lie still," he wrote himself,
"from patience Death will bloom."

The Fall

Sorry I dripped blood on your shoes.
I fell over the ladder in the garage
while carrying a knife. Blood gushed
out of my finger like a forest spring.
As I rose from a cold gray cement I saw
your shoes receive it as a gift. a cloud burst
of red on their barren gray.

Standing before me now in your shadow
as you show the stain, I taste a bitter fruit.
Forgive my carelessness shed on you.
It is no true measure of my love.

Long Nights

Clock radio beside my brother's bed
earthquake lines in the ceiling
until the lights go off and I
wrap the covers tight between my legs.

Old houses lean toward mills
green hedges guiding in and out
tubs of gray ashes hauled to the alley
where catholic schoolgirls walk.

Cold black windows glare as
skims of headlights cross the walls.
All we do not speak of
dances into our dreams.

Wages

Payday comes in from the cold
and sets a bag down in the hallway.
She finds her place at the table
where we are dressed in our good clothes.
Mom is already drinking wine
and Dad is telling funny work stories.
Payday's laugh is like coins falling on a metal tray.
We pass her the pork chops
and watch her fork not one, but two.
"One for later," she grins at us, and
like always we pretend to smile.

By the time the sun has set
we've said good-bye to our Payday
and a silence fills the room.
When I break a plate, Mom cries out,
"Oh, dear God! Look what you've done."
A train roars by in the wind.
Then Mom hands Dad a fist of bills,
and we kids go off to our rooms.
Tomorrow will mean our old clothes again
and the counting of our coins.

The Millyard

Watching from millyard bench
as the lace shadows of fire escape
inch down the long brick wall,
I breathe in the hot air
await the sun's release.

Young red-haired woman
wearing tin-mill blue carries
a lunch pail against her breasts.
Beyond lewd calls of track crew,
she tucks her children into bed.

"College boys" they call us
and give us shit jobs
refusing to learn our names.
Yet their shower-room bodies
gleam like new iron girders.

With others at the time clock
we stand card in hand
await the next click.
The old guy I worked with
lives right across the street
above the bar.

A Work Story

"A good man is hard to find."

Work shows up one day
red faced with lunch pail
and takes a seat at the bar.
I ask, "What'll you have?" And he,
"What you need done?"

Four days later the new kitchen is finished
shining chrome and real tile floor.
I tell him he can have free drinks
for as long as he lives, and he laughs,
says, "Hey, the job ain't done."

When I get home that night,
Work is sitting on the porch
and says, "I've come for that drink
and to sleep with your wife."
I laugh, but he doesn't.

He's fixed the porch now
and put in a new furnace,
while I just drive the kids to school
and sleep on the couch. This weekend
he and Grace are heading to Vegas.

Visit to the Hungarian Museum

You enter by a signature and a sample of your blood,
then bow your head. Bright colors everywhere…
robes and scarves draped, plates and cups totter on shelves,
beside the hair canteens and shiny sabers
for slicing off heads and arms.
Fine Hungarian wolf hounds guide you
past photo lineups of the rich and famous,
Hungarians who've invented everything.
Old books are stacked like leaves of cabbage.

And in the back room lined against the walls
are the old Hungarians who smile at you;
the women's faces are long, the men's are round.
They speak in a tongue of twisted alphabet,
retelling stories of the white stag and the golden crown,
and how their families made a life in America.
They tell of their food and music:
paprika and poppy seeds again and again,
as well as the waltz and the polkazok.
They are so happy to share their past; they smile
and never mention the Jews and the Gypsies
murdered by their countrymen.

Finally, two fair-faced children dressed only in white
usher you to the door again, where the boy
taps you on each shoulder with a *Kolachi* nut roll.
The girl stuffs a Kafli cookie into your mouth, says,
"Swallow it at once." Then both whisper *Viszlat*,
and you hear yourself answer *köszönöm*,
then smile, your head bowed as you leave.

The Passage

The ship docks on a foreign shore where even the gulls deny your name. You and other passengers carry bags up the gangway into the new world.

With passport hung like a sandwich round your neck, your feet planted on fresh earth, the too ripe smell of fish inside your nose, you smile unknowingly.

It is said your ancestors may have come from here, this island in the middle of the sea. Here you must greet yourself and walk toward the sound of old buildings in a square.

Do the faces look like yours? Do they move and gesture like your grandfather's who died when you were four? All you have is a name like his when he first came to America.

At the city center you find a small café facing the marketplace where words bubble up like scrambled eggs. Here you sit at a table drinking cup after cup of coffee while watching the old woman wrap loaves of bread in brown paper, the young busboy wipe tables with a wet cloth, the old man puff on a white clay pipe, pretty girls in bright skirts laugh while passing by.

All day you sit waiting and watching for your past to arrive.

Enter Stranger

A door-to-door salesman has come to our house. Mom opens the door a crack as Dave and I gather at her waist. A young man or older boy is standing there, and with a shaky voice, says, "Magazines, Mam, is what I'm selling." We look to each other. "Can I come in for a moment?" he asks sliding round the door.

Mom introduces us, and we grin while he rustles his papers. "Yes," he says, "that's good." We are all crowded in our hallway when he blurts out, "Oh, I hate to ask, Mam, but could I please use your bathroom?" Mom looks at us for some answer to this, but we just shrug. "Yes," she finally says, and we boys lead him up the stairs, then hear the bathroom door latch and lock.

He is in there still and won't come out. We hear the bath water running. When we call, he just groans like a dog. As we look around our old hallway it has become somehow strange. His world has become ours and transformed it, like when a movie first starts at the show. "Please come out," Mom cries to him. Nothing. She goes to the phone in her bedroom. We stare at the bathroom door.

Uncle Ray is downstairs now and he's brought two policemen into our house. Our upstairs welcomes strangeness again. An officer pounds on the bathroom door ordering the man-boy to open. Mom moves us boys into our bedroom where we can still watch our stranger come out, his head bowed his body a prisoner now. He gives us boys one wild look then disappears down the stairs.

Breathless, as if struck hard in the chest or waking inside of a dream, we shake our heads in wonder. I ask if we'll be on the news?

Mom says, "I don't know, but just wait till your father gets home."

Elvis Resurrection

By the time they pack us up again, I'm ready to move. Five years boxed, standing up in an old warehouse—it's about time. Hey, how is that to treat a king! King of Rock that is—"Elvis in the warehouse," the other dummies joke. But I always knew that one day I'd be back on top, showman that I am, featuring at some classy New York museum or Vegas casino. Word is, a bunch of us from Niagara's old "Celebrities in Wax House" are being moved to the Midwest. Not my choice, but, hey, Elvis is big everywhere. We stars, Liz and Liza, Bogie and Bacall, Kennedy and Nixon, and a bunch of others are all being loaded up. We'll need a supporting cast.

The train ride is pretty dull, but that's normal for us who stand and wait outside any concept of time. Like horses and cattle, we sleep standing up. If they lay us down, see, we begin to sag and warp. You don't want that and neither do I. Believe me.

At the station in Cleveland we're loaded onto a freight truck. I can see through the cracks and hear the workers cursing the lifting. Little do they know whom they handle—the famous transported in the back of a truck. Pretty ironic. But I do understand such security measures. People always want to touch me or worse, and there was that awful woman in Niagara.

When the truck finally stops, the doors slide up. The light hits us, and all I can see is a big red brick building with the words "Silver Lining Cathedral" in big white letters. My name's not yet reached the marquee or billboards. The workers unload us onto dollies, and suddenly another group of buildings appear, probably our trailers near the set. Once inside, we are stripped down, our show garments exchanged for costumes, my gold lame folded on a chair. Naked in wax, nothing really moves or matters. Let them look. I was made to show it all, with all my anatomy clearly intact. The costume women look up and giggle as they unwrap a long cloth, a robe it seems…for the King. But why such humble cloth? It seems ancient and common, yet, as they say, "Anything for the film." At first a hood comes over my head, then wisely someone allows my face to be seen. "Never hide your star."

I'm being carried into a room with three walls, our set no doubt. Others are standing robed before me assembled in waiting before a gray-blue sky with a lightning streak. There's Natalie over there kneeling with Jennifer by the rocks. Edward G. and Vincent are holding long, pointed spears. I'm waiting for my blocking when the director calls out something, and my robe is taken off, my arms are being raised and carefully reattached. I am the figure to be placed— up there in the light. My God! Oh, my God. It's the cross!

As wounds are being painted on my legs and hands, I think of Mother, and a beautiful smile comes over my face. I feel it—we are, all us, in a Bible wax museum.

Winter

"Some poems are written with the eyes open
and some with the eyes closed."
                    ~Charles Simic

white bones clack in late dawn
trees sing of places they have never been
blackbirds count the inches of snow
in the distance of afternoon
a silence bites the skin
windows freeze at dusk and we
count our friends on one hand

our coats become our lovers
our gloves are dark tattoos
our shoes are feet now
our breath a piece of melting ice
frozen milk jugs on door steps salute:
"Welcome to the storm."

What's There

I throw open these double doors
and am stunned by the emptiness—
nothing but an endless drop.

I throw up a road block—"Danger—Do Not Pass"
and return to my work, putting space
between myself and this.

No dragons, no devils, and not
the face of God—just "This"
endless blur of good and evil.

Listen to the silence roar.
Search the dark for signs of light.
Close eyes, open heart to self.

Part Three

Open the Eyes of My Heart...

~Paul Baloche

Inside these Woods

smoke rises with the light
against the dark of trees
their legs and arms stretched
to embrace our rite of burning logs

too many days spent wiping spit
and bending backs to not release now
accept the smell against the skin
inside our weathered clothes

our parents gone inside the darkness
leaving us to breathe alone
to welcome the warmth within

Dandelion Resurrection

Four workers lay cement squares in the grass
making a pathway around the building.
It's their job, and they need the work.
While birds gather in the trees to watch,
cement slabs settle down on #3 fill,
to be leveled by human hands.

All flora and fauna are crushed down
erasing the dandelions of spring.
Or so they think, till May's middle
when green stems curve round
these cold gray blocks,
and a bright yellow stretches up
silent in the sun.

Woman's Work

Above me a woman walks a tight-rope
in sequenced leotard—scales of green
above a tight black bottom.
Below a pool of snakes swirl as she throws
herself upon the line then bounces back
amidst our hail of gasps then applause.

Elephants dance, tigers roar, cyclists
circle a cage, and there she stands near clowns,
already forgotten yet holding the rope
that keeps the tent up. Now she's ushering
us peasants to our cars. Her face
more beautiful than the stars.

Women's Hair

smoke rising from a campfire
deep scent of the seasons
sugar sprinkled on bread and butter
fingers interlacing hands
threads woven into a scarf of
black and red, brown and yellow
silk against the face
french curves inside themselves
dangling at the breasts
a crest of tender nakedness
touch the soul, kiss the sky
sweet Marys in a glass of wine

The Kiss

Tender sharing of the breath
eyes closed then open
to the glory of the face
embraced by trusted hands.

So too this sharing comes
in meditation as in prayer
intimate focus—self and other
held as one in lotus.

Arms up toward sun
then down to touch of earth.
Each breath—this life
taken in then released.

A train passes through our stillness
each affecting the other
till all movement is one—
a sharing of the breath.

The Dance

with one hand she lifts her skirt
a rose within a garden
the other strokes her bare breasts
spheres turning in moonlight.

now her arms beckon you
the music of her hair
draws you from your seat.

you remove your shirt
your lips are touching hers
sweet exchange of breath
tongues aflame with light

now you are dancing too

The Dress

The dress speaks of better times
when everything fit and belonged.
"I've covered your skin and held you close."
"Those days are gone," the woman says,
"and soon, so will you." The dress
just hangs there awaiting the next move,
to be pulled down and shoved into a plastic bag
headed for the trash or the Goodwill box,
the way of so many others.

Looking herself over, she sees few flaws,
no buttons missing, nor zippers snagged.
"I've kept myself well," she declares, "though yes,
we've aged." Then facing the woman,
 asks, "Oh, Grace, what's happened to you?"
But the woman has already turned away,
working to slip into that short leather skirt.
"Christ, you're a woman, not a teen," calls the dress.
Silence, then almost in tears, "I'd hoped to be around
to see you love yourself."

The dress just hangs there waiting,
then feels the woman's hand
pull her down from the rack.

If Not For

If it were not for your laughter
our shadows would disappear
in the leaves by the road.

If it were not for your hands
my heart would fall from the sky
a dark and leaden bird.

If it were not for your lips
our words would turn to
mute piles of stones.

If it were not for your breath
my own would stop cold
death planted in my chest.

I reach over to your warm body
plant kisses along your neck
await the song of your eyes.

Night Vision

Someone comes in without knocking
placing their shoes by the door
someone so help me is here now.
Well, what shall I do?
I rise from bed and grab a club,
but there in the hall is an old face
I struggle to recall. *Joyce*
it is Joy of my youth
aged now like an orange.
She smiles and whispers
"I've come to tell you something."
What can it be?
"I've loved you from afar."
But why my face asks.
"Listen now, our mothers were friends."
I nod into her wet eyes. "But our fathers
were one and the same." I bow,
I breathe, I look up and she is gone
turned into smoke, and I in my dreams.

Lost and Found

I am calling the restaurant this morning
to see if they've found my sense of humor
which I lost with my appetite last night.
They are checking the lost and found.

I had been eating their Cesare Salad
when friends began talking of politics—
what's wrong and how they can do nothing.
With a meatball just touching my lips
the talk turned to today's religions.

The woman who answered now is checking the drawer.
"Where were you sitting?" she asks. I tell her, and
they are sending someone back to check. In this long
pause, I ask, "What else do you have in that box?"
She almost laughs, "Oh, a scarf, a pair of gloves,
two credit cards, and three memories—
did you lose any of that?" she asks.
I hold silence a long time wondering why I called,
and then I ask, "What size are the gloves?"

Taste of Age

lick the lips, then swallow
the moldy crust of my ham sandwich
bending with tree limbs in wind
racoons reaching the sky beside the road
voices rumbling underwater
closet shoes telling me old stories
backing my last car with eyes closed
tracing aches like moles into holes
pretending to be friends yet plotting murder

the moments slide down the throat
following that woman to the wrong car
who's that in the photo or the mirror?
holding words in my lap like rocks
unfinished books leading away from the grave
praying to be safe not sorry
forgetting why I called
pretending to be listening to all this

Dog Archeology

The dog runs off in a field.
Under wild bushes he releases
mementos for all ages.
May they turn to stone.

He glances into its face, turns
then scuffs at his earth deposit.
Let them place it in a case one day
trace it back to my diet.

For a while he chases birds
barks his name at their tails.
I have no wings, just pray that one day
they will read my bones right.

The wind rustles his fur,
he barks into the air.
Life is simple here
where we are what we are.

The Cold

You are on an old Greyhound bus
and the driver has left open the door
so that wind rushes in to fill the frigid space.
Your shoulders are hunched like a lama's
and your hands squeezed like fish between your legs.
The old woman on your right has already died
but you all keep smiling, believing a god
will end this ride toward hell.

Frost on your eye lashes can freeze
and seal your eyes shut, so you blink,
and blink, and blink again.
Cold burns inside your chest.
You can't breathe and will soon die.
Suddenly the driver stops to piss in a bottle
and you jump off, make a run for it.
Snow smacking your face into a blur
you see a light, a road, and then a house.
You fall again and again yet find yourself
standing there, knocking, waiting
your prayer now just a hum. The door opens
and you fall forward at their feet.

Weather Report

soft soprano voices
landing at the window
light touching light

boat sailing lake waters
with no one aboard
but three gulls

fish on the line
kite in the sky
skating over ice

leaves turning
with our souls
lost in wind

invisible borders
rise in the mind
walling the heart

oh, please, feed the wolves.

The Call

wordless flutter of wings nearby
widowed call of wild goose
blind night sky above
peasant earth holding below

eyes close on a vision of fish
swimming through blue air
single yet whole
empty yet full

off in the distance
the roar then rumble
of a train leaving home

No Walls

Where is the wall that can hold us
keep us from each other's love?
Artifice is nothing before spirit
mind melted by heart.
Dogs bark at its corners
bay at rocks stacked high,
cement poured into would-be tombs.
Birds fly over, creatures dig under,
people reach through and around.
We paint its face, tear it down by night.
Sun, moon, and stars deny it.
O, where is the wall that can hold us,
keep us from each other's love?

Yoga Bake

We've come a long way to be with ourselves,

lying here colored mats over hardwood floors,
the room full of sun swept bodies,
legs and bottoms wrapped handsome tight.

We've reached and stretched, lifted and crossed,
kissing pain with the word—"Enjoy"
as we bend—dog prone—
feet and shoulders burning.
In silence we do all that is asked.

Our age dissolves inside us, as we slow dance;
we rest, we sweat, breathe in and out,
greet our new selves rising.

8:45 a.m. Café

"I've forgotten more than I ever knew," the old man said to himself, but loud enough for his friends to hear something. Seated around a breakfast table they were drinking cup after cup of coffee served by the waitress acting as their mother or old girl friend, calling each of them honey or sweetie or dear.

The old man had been staring down into his eggs over-easy for so long they seemed like eyes looking back into him.

"What?" the waitress asked.

"Oh," he looked up at her face which seemed newly kind. "Nothing...I was just mumbling to myself."

"No, go on, say it again for us all to hear," said his friend Paul.

There came a moment when the forks were held or set down, a silence almost religious. He looked round the table of faces, and it came out again, "I feel I've forgotten more than I ever knew."

Some smiled almost laughing, some shook their heads, and some nodded, for they were all on that road.

And then the waitress began to pour another round, but this time touching each man on the shoulder or arm, and finally saying, "Oh my, guys, this world is much more than we'll ever know."

The Caring

You reach into my wound
and cannot take your hand away.
A cardinal sings of this
to all with ears and eyes.
I too am moved to song.

Touch, the vibrant wand,
my eyes there in yours,
our breath becoming one.
Inside the silence of moments
our hands are washed with light.

"I Shall Be Released"

Too many and too much
knocking at my front door
phone ringing inside my head
days of dollars and doldrums.

Let all words cease, empty out.
Fold into a blanket of music
cresting over and around.
Lie back and breathe deep
one hundred thousand times.

Eyes closed and naked free
let birds feed on your feet.
Earth, wind, and sky,
release all that you carry.
You are the distant whistle of the train.
You are the river of your dreams.

Author photo by Ann Smith

Larry Smith is a native of the industrial Ohio River Valley having grown up in Mingo Junction, Ohio., the second of four children. His father was a brakeman on the railroad of Weirton Steel where the author worked two summers to help pay for college. A graduate of Mingo High School, Muskingum College, and Kent State University, he taught at Bowling Green State University's Firelands College from 1970 to 2012.

He is the author of eight previous books of poetry, two books of memoirs, five books of fiction, two literary biographies of authors Lawrence Ferlinghetti and Kenneth Patchen, and two books of poetry translations from the Chinese. Smith has received fellowships from the Ohio Arts Council and the National Endowment for the Humanities and was a Fulbright Lecturer in Italy from 1980 to 1981. His photo history of his hometown Mingo Junction, Ohio appeared in Arcadia's Images of America Series. Two of his film scripts on authors James Wright and Kenneth Patchen have been made into films with his co-director Tom Koba. He was the first poet laureate of Huron, Ohio.

Larry is the founder and director of The Firelands Writing Center and a co-founder with his wife, Ann, of Converging Paths Meditation Center in Huron, Ohio. He and his wife live along the sandy shores of Lake Erie in Huron, Ohio, and are parents of three adults and eight grandchildren.

BOOKS BY BOTTOM DOG PRESS
Harmony Series

The Pears by Larry Smith 62 pgs. $12

Without a Plea by Jeff Gundy 96 pgs. $16

What Burden Do Those Trains Bear Away, by Kathleen S. Burgess 96 pgs. $16

Taking a Walk in My Animal Hat, by Charlene Fix, 90 pgs, $16

Earnest Occupations, by Richard Hague, 200 pgs, $18

Pieces: A Composite Novel, by Mary Ann McGuigan, 250 pgs, $18

Crows in the Jukebox: Poems, by Mike James, 106 pgs, $16

Portrait of the Artist as a Bingo Worker: by Lori Jakiela, 216 pgs, $18

The Thick of Thin: A Memoir, by Larry Smith, 238 pgs, $18

Cold Air Return: Novel, by Patrick Lawrence O'Keeffe, 390 pgs, $20

Flesh and Stones: A Memoir, by Jan Shoemaker, 176 pgs, $18

Waiting to Begin: A Memoir by Patricia O'Donnell, 166 pgs, $18

And Waking: Poems by Kevin Casey, 80 pgs, $16

Both Shoes Off: Poems by Jeanne Bryner, 112 pgs, $16

Abandoned Homeland: Poems by Jeff Gundy, 96 pgs, $16

Stolen Child: A Novel by Suzanne Kelly, 338 pgs, $18

On the Flyleaf: Poems by Herbert Woodward Martin, 106 pgs, $16

The Harmonist at Nightfall: Poems by Shari Wagner, 114 pgs, $16

Painting Bridges: A Novel by Patricia Averbach, 234 pgs, $18

Ariadne & Other Poems by Ingrid Swanberg, 120 pgs, $16

The Search for the Reason Why: Poems by Tom Kryss, 192 pgs, $16

Kenneth Patchen: Rebel Poet in America by Larry Smith, Revised 2nd Edition, 326 pgs, Cloth $28

Selected Correspondence of Kenneth Patchen, Edited with introduction by Allen Frost, Paper $18/ Cloth $28

Awash with Roses: Collected Love Poems of Kenneth Patchen Eds. Laura Smith and Larry Smith 200 pgs, $16

Breathing the West: Poems by Liane Ellison Norman, 96 pgs, $16

Maggot: A Novel by Robert Flanagan, 262 pgs, $18

American Poet: A Novel by Jeff Vande Zande, 200 pgs, $18

The Way-Back Room: Memoir of a Detroit Childhood by Mary Minock, 216 pgs, $18

Echo: Poems by Christina Lovin 86 pgs. $16

Bottom Dog Press http://smithdocs.net

www.ingramcontent.com/pod-product-compliance
Lightning Source LLC
Chambersburg PA
CBHW020732250626
47155CB00006B/2263